I0780612

Time Empowered

10 Golden Rules for Transforming Your Calendar and Productivity

*"Transform your calendar from chaos to clarity,
your journey to empowered scheduling starts here."*

Abimbola Oshodi

Copyright © 2025 Abimbola Oshodi

All rights reserved.

TABLE OF CONTENTS

ACKNOWLEDGMENTS

Creating "*Time Empowered: 10 Rules for Transforming Your Calendar & Productivity*" has been a rewarding journey, and I am deeply grateful to God Almighty for giving me the vision that I can write a book, and most especially, the inspiration He gave me during the development process of this book.

First, I am grateful to my Pastor, Apostle Tomi Abayomi of Rig Global Church, for the mentorship and the invaluable knowledge, I continually receive from his teachings, his words really made it possible for the vision to come to realization. I also would like to use this opportunity to say a big thank you to Apostle Peter and Prophetess Andrea of Rig London, the words you spoke over my life is beginning to manifest, and this book is a testament of it, God bless you both.

I express my heartfelt appreciation to my wonderful son, David, who has been nothing but a pillar of support, his unwavering encouragement, patience, and understanding sustained me throughout the writing and development process.

I also extend my sincere gratitude to my former Boss Tracey Ann Burgess: Trace you gave me the opportunity to be not just your Executive Assistant, but you offered me the platform that helped provide most of the valuable insights that inspired the content of this book. Your commitment to empowering people and enhancing productivity continually motivates me.

I would like to acknowledge, Eniola Yakubu; thank you for tightening all the loose ends and for making sure everything runs smoothly, I appreciate you.

Lastly, special thanks to you, the reader, for choosing this book. Your dedication to personal and professional growth inspires me daily. May this book empower you to reclaim your time and live a life of purpose and clarity.

Introduction

Have you ever felt overwhelmed by meetings that never seem to end, overlapping appointments, or busy working days, yet no real accomplishments? Your calendar should be an empowerment tool rather than be your biggest obstacle. What if your calendar could become your greatest ally, and unlock new levels of productivity, clarity, and professional fulfillment? Welcome to Time Empowered: 10 Golden Rules for transforming your calendar & productivity, your guide to reclaiming control of your time and transforming your daily routine into a seamless pathway to success.

In today's fast, paced world, mastering your calendar isn't simply about avoiding scheduling conflicts, it's about prioritizing effectively, creating intentional space for strategic thinking, and finding a balance between your personal and professional life. In this book, you'll uncover ten powerful, yet practical rules designed to help you streamline your schedule, eliminate overwhelm, and ensure every appointment serves your broader goals. Each rule is rooted in real, world wisdom and actionable insights that elite executive assistants and professionals rely upon daily to achieve outstanding results.

Prepare to revolutionize your approach to scheduling. By the end of this guide, you'll no longer view your calendar as a source of stress, but rather as your secret weapon for achieving high productivity and fulfillment. If you're ready to stop merely surviving your schedule and start mastering your moments, turn the page, your journey to calendar mastery begins now.

Chapter 1

Rule 1

Protect Your Time Like Crown Jewels

Have you ever paused to consider that your time is the most valuable asset, arguably more precious than gold, diamonds, or any material wealth? Unlike money, once your time is spent, it's irrevocably gone. As an executive assistant or a busy professional, your effectiveness hinges upon your ability to respect and protect this invaluable resource. Protecting your time isn't merely a nice, to, have; it's the cornerstone of professional excellence and personal well, being.

However, in a demanding work environment, your calendar can easily become prey to "time hijackers," those seemingly minor interruptions and unnecessary meetings that cumulatively rob hours from your day. Identifying these hijackers is your first step toward reclaiming control. Whether it's colleagues who habitually drop by unannounced, last, minute invitations to meetings lacking clear agendas, or even your own temptation to multitask ineffectively, pinpointing these culprits enables you to erect protective boundaries around your schedule.

Saying "no" is an essential skill, but mastering how to say it with grace is equally crucial. In the professional world, you might fear that declining requests or invitations might label you as uncooperative or unhelpful. Yet, the truth is quite the opposite. Those who protect their calendars effectively are viewed as decisive and respectful of both their own and others' commitments. In this chapter, you'll discover practical scripts and strategies to confidently and politely decline interruptions and unnecessary requests, thus preserving your schedule without straining relationships.

Creating a robust system of boundaries around your time means intentionally setting aside space for what truly matters. This involves evaluating tasks, appointments, and activities to determine if they're aligned with your core objectives and personal values. When you prioritize effectively, you're signaling to others, and yourself, that your time is both purposeful and non, negotiable. We'll explore how to clearly communicate these boundaries to your colleagues, ensuring everyone respects the sanctity of your time.

Moreover, safeguarding your calendar involves proactive habits. Engaging in routines such as calendar audits: regular review of your schedule to identify and eliminate unproductive activities is a game, changing practice. Imagine the clarity you'll gain by periodically asking yourself, "Does this meeting or appointment serve a clear purpose aligned with my goals?" Such vigilance prevents calendar bloat, reduces stress, and frees you to invest energy into tasks with high impact and real meaning.

Ultimately, protecting your time like crown jewels transforms your relationship with your calendar from one of overwhelm and obligation to empowerment and intentionality. It fosters a professional image of strength and reliability, enhancing your reputation and productivity. This chapter sets the foundation for calendar mastery by empowering you to treat your time with the respect it truly deserves. Remember, when you safeguard your time, you safeguard your success, professionally and personally.

Checklist

Identify Your Time Hijackers:

- List recurring interruptions you commonly face (e.g., unnecessary meetings, last, minute requests, phone calls, or emails).

- Note how often these interruptions occur and the amount of productive time they consume.

Clearly Define Your Boundaries:

- Establish your daily "protected time slots" dedicated exclusively to critical tasks.

- Communicate your availability clearly with your colleagues or team members.

Master the Art of Saying "No" Gracefully:

- Develop a polite, professional template for declining meetings or tasks that don't align with your goals.

- Practice your scripts for declining requests, ensuring clarity and kindness in your delivery.

Prioritize Your Tasks:

- Clearly define your high, value activities, tasks directly aligned with your primary goals.

- Allocate and block specific times each day for these high, priority tasks.

Conduct Regular Calendar Audits:

- Schedule weekly calendar audits to review upcoming appointments and commitments.

- Identify and eliminate or reschedule any meetings or tasks that aren't aligned with your core objectives.

Set Up Defensive Scheduling:

- Schedule intentional buffer times around important meetings to avoid feeling rushed or pressured.

- Block dedicated "Do Not Disturb" periods daily to maintain uninterrupted productivity.

Cultivate a Culture of Respectful Communication

- Clearly inform coworkers or stakeholders about your schedule preferences (e.g., preferred meeting durations, advance notice).

- Establish protocols for urgent vs. non, urgent communication, reducing unnecessary interruptions.

Leverage Technology to Guard Your Time:

- Activate digital "Do Not Disturb" functions or focus modes during protected times.

- Utilize calendar management apps or integrations to automatically enforce your availability preferences.

Reflect and Adjust Regularly:

- Evaluate how effectively you maintain your boundaries.

- Adjust your strategies based on what worked well and what needs improvement.

Celebrate and Reinforce Your Success:

- Reward yourself for successfully protecting your time each week.

- Share positive experiences and techniques with colleagues to foster mutual respect and understanding of time protection.

Chapter 2

Rule 2

Prioritize & Time Block

If time is currency, then prioritization is your spending strategy. Many professionals make the mistake of assuming that busy equals productivity. The reality, however, often reveals a different story, days filled with frantic activities that yield minimal progress toward meaningful goals. Effective prioritization empowers you to distinguish between the merely urgent and genuinely important. It's about understanding that while many tasks demand your attention, only a select few deserve your focused energy.

The power of prioritization begins with clarity. To determine what truly matters, you must first identify and articulate your key professional objectives and personal values. Ask yourself: "Which tasks contribute directly to achieving my strategic goals? Which tasks offer the greatest return on investment?" This chapter equips you with actionable frameworks, such as the Eisenhower Matrix, a powerful tool to categorize tasks by urgency and importance. When used effectively, these methods transform chaotic days into purposeful pursuits, ensuring your schedule always aligns with your highest priorities.

Prioritizing alone isn't enough, you need a structured system to execute consistently. This is where time blocking comes into play. Time blocking is a proven scheduling method that involves dedicating specific blocks of time to individual tasks or categories of work, thus eliminating ambiguity and distractions. Imagine each task or project as a meeting with yourself, non, negotiable and strictly respected. We'll dive deeply into how you can leverage this technique, from setting realistic durations to strategically aligning high, priority tasks during your peak productivity hours.

The secret to effective time blocking lies in realistic scheduling and disciplined execution. Many professionals mistakenly overload their schedules with back, to, back tasks, leaving no margin for unforeseen events or essential breaks. To avoid falling into this trap, this chapter offers guidance on accurately estimating task durations and strategically positioning your time blocks. You'll also discover how leaving intentional gaps in your schedule can serve as critical buffers to maintain productivity and mental clarity, allowing you to adapt gracefully when unexpected challenges arise.

Another pivotal aspect of mastering prioritization and time blocking is communicating your boundaries clearly to your colleagues and stakeholders. Transparency about your availability fosters mutual respect, reduces misunderstandings, and allows your coworkers to adapt to your time management system seamlessly. We'll discuss practical tips and effective communication scripts to gently but firmly inform others of your schedule constraints, empowering you to maintain the integrity of your carefully designed calendar.

Moreover, embracing prioritization and time blocking encourages deep work, dedicated periods of uninterrupted focus essential for achieving high, quality outcomes. In an era dominated by multitasking and constant digital interruptions, deep work is becoming increasingly rare yet ever more valuable. In this section, you'll learn practical strategies to create and protect deep work sessions, ensuring you produce your best work consistently and efficiently.

In essence, prioritization and time blocking work in harmony to transform your professional life from reactive to proactive. Mastering these skills enables you not only to accomplish more but also to accomplish what truly matters. By implementing the insights and practical exercises outlined in this chapter, you will confidently take charge of your daily schedule, dramatically boosting your productivity, effectiveness, and professional satisfaction. Get ready, because once you experience the clarity and empowerment these strategies provide, you'll never manage your time the same way again

Checklist

PRIORITIZATION CHECKPOINTS

Identify Your Top 3 Priorities for the Week

- What must be accomplished to move your goals forward?

- Are they aligned with your core responsibilities and long, term vision?

Use the Eisenhower Matrix

- Categorize tasks: Urgent/Important | Not Urgent/Important | Urgent/Not Important | Not Urgent/Not Important.

- Eliminate or delegate low, value tasks from your calendar.

Define Your 'Non, Negotiables'

- What activities or meetings cannot be compromised (e.g., strategy sessions, client deliverables, personal recharge)?

- Are you honoring your most important work?

Clarify Outcome, Not Just Activity

- Have you clearly outlined what "done" looks like for each task?

- Are you focusing on results rather than just being busy?

TIME BLOCKING STRATEGY CHECKPOINTS

Assigning Blocks for Deep Work

- Reserve uninterrupted time (60–90 mins) for high, focus tasks.

- Add labels like "Creative Work," "Planning," or "Strategic Thinking" to your calendar.

Schedule Admin & Routine Tasks

- Create small blocks (15–30 mins) for emails, reports, and updates.

- Use batching to group similar low, effort tasks together.

Add White Space for Transitions

- Include 10–15, minute gaps between meetings or tasks.

- Avoid mental fatigue by giving your brain room to reset.

Protect Personal Time

- Have you blocked time for meals, breaks, prayers, or family?

- Are you honoring rest and restoration as essential, not optional?

REVIEW & REFINE

Conduct Weekly Review

- What worked well with your prioritization?

- Where did you over, commit, or under, plan?

Adjust as Needed

- Are your blocks realistic and flexible?

- Have you built space to shift tasks if needed?

Chapter 3

Rule 3

Create Buffer Time & Avoid Overload

Have you ever faced a day so tightly scheduled that the mere thought of a delay sends shivers down your spine? We've all been there racing from one meeting to the next, constantly checking the clock, and feeling like your schedule controls you, rather than the other way around. The truth is, relentless back, to, back scheduling doesn't lead to productivity; instead, it results in burnout, mistakes, and stress. This chapter introduces a crucial strategy to reverse that cycle: the concept of buffer time.

So, what exactly is buffer time, and why is it essential? Simply put, buffer time refers to strategically placed gaps within your schedule, small windows of unscheduled time that serve as breathing space between meetings or tasks. Think of buffer time as the shock absorbers in a vehicle, cushioning your schedule against inevitable disruptions, transitions, or unexpected emergencies. These gaps aren't signs of idleness; they're signs of wisdom and foresight, ensuring that you're always operating at your best.

Creating effective buffer time starts with intentional planning. In this chapter, we'll guide you through practical methods to determine how much buffer time you genuinely need. You'll engage in a reflective exercise to evaluate past scheduling challenges when you wished you had an extra few minute. By learning from past experiences, you can accurately forecast your buffer requirements and strategically insert these essential pauses into your daily schedule.

Beyond merely avoiding overload, buffer times can dramatically enhance your productivity and creativity. Imagine finishing a task or meeting with sufficient time to regroup, process information, and plan thoughtfully for what's next. You'll discover in this chapter that these brief periods of pause often lead to sharper decision, making, improved cognitive performance, and enhanced emotional well, being. We'll explore real, world scenarios demonstrating how leaders use buffer time not just to relax, but to optimize their effectiveness throughout the day.

Now, let's get interactive! As you read, you'll be prompted to try a practical "buffer challenge." In this hands, on activity, you'll deliberately schedule buffer times for your next working week, guided by easy, to, follow templates and checklists provided in this chapter. You'll document your experiences, noting shifts in your stress levels, performance, and overall job satisfaction. This interactive element ensures you don't just learn about buffer time, in theory, you'll experience its profound benefits firsthand.

But buffer time isn't only for recovering from meetings or tasks; it's also critical for personal well, being. We'll delve into the importance of short breaks for mental health, energy renewal, and maintaining a positive outlook in your professional environment. This section highlights easy, to, adopt activities for your buffer times, such as brief mindfulness exercises, stretching routines, or even quick, uplifting interactions with colleagues, fostering a balanced and harmonious working environment.

Ultimately, by embracing buffer time, you're choosing sustainability over short, lived intensity, quality over quantity, and calmness over chaos. The strategies outlined in this chapter will empower you to reclaim control over your schedule, creating a workday that feels manageable and fulfilling rather than exhausting. It's time to let go of the pressure, filled illusion of non, stop productivity and step into a smarter, healthier approach, one where your productivity thrives because your well, being is prioritized. Ready to regain your rhythm? Let's dive in and start buffering your way to brilliance.

Checklist

Create space. Preserve energy. Work smarter, not faster.

Rethink the "Back, to, Back" Mindset

"Productivity is not about doing more, it's about doing what matters without burning out."

- Remove at least one back, to, back meeting from today's schedule.

- Review my week and spot any overloaded days that need rebalancing.

- Understand that availability ≠ effectiveness, I've protected focus over face time.

Reflection Prompt:

Is there one meeting today I can shorten, move, or remove to protect my energy?

Built in Breathing Room

"You can't extract from an empty calendar."

- Add **at least 10 minutes** between major meetings today.

- Include a midday pause for lunch, stretch, or mindful breathing.

- I've scheduled mental reset time before any high, stakes session or decision, making meeting.

Action Step:

Use the 10/50 rule: For every hour of work, allow **10 minutes of pause.**

Apply Smart Buffering Techniques

"Spacing out your schedule is not laziness, it's rulership."

- I've color, coded my **buffer zones** (ex: gray or light

blue) so they stand out.

- I've used calendar notes to label breaks with specific intentions (walk, reflect, prep, review).
- I've set a recurring 15, min daily wrap, up time to reflect and plan tomorrow.

Useful Tip:

Use phrases like *"Executive Reset"* or *"Transition Prep"* to emphasize buffer time to others.

Maintain Sustainable Productivity

"Pace isn't everything, **consistency** wins the long game."

- I've reviewed my energy highs and lows and scheduled tasks accordingly.
- I've set at least one hour today for deep work, no distractions, no multitasking.
- I've planned at least one non, work mini joy break (walk, music, snack, journaling).

Energy Gauge Check, In:

On a scale of 1, 10, how energized do I feel right now?

 __/10

Bonus Action:

Repeat to yourself:

"My schedule reflects my priorities. I protect my peace so I can perform with power."

Chapter 4

Rule 4

Proactive Conflict Resolution

Spotting and Solving Schedule Clashes Before They Erupt

In the world of calendar management, conflict is not always loud, it often creeps in quietly through overlapping meetings, misunderstood priorities, or double, bookings that slowly chip away at your credibility and your executive's peace of mind. Proactive conflict resolution is the art of identifying these quiet conflicts before they explode into full, blown chaos. A well, managed calendar doesn't just keep time; it keeps the peace. The secret lies in developing foresight, training your eyes to see the friction points that others may miss. Whether it's a routine clash between two high, stakes meetings or tension brewing between personal commitments and professional demands, your role is to be the silent strategist who ensures the day flows like a well, rehearsed symphony.

A powerful first step is developing a keen eye for potential friction. This means regularly scanning your calendar not just a day in advance, but a week or two ahead, to identify time overlaps, back, to, back commitments without breaks, or meetings that may run over. Are there two executives vying for the same time slot? Is a board meeting bumping too close to your executive's presentation prep time? A well, trained calendar manager thinks like a chess player. The more you anticipate, the less you'll need to apologize for. When you're consistently ahead of schedule clashes, you build a reputation not just for punctuality but for protecting the sanity and rhythm of your workplace.

But spotting is only half the problem. Once a conflict is identified, the next step is **strategic negotiation**. This doesn't always involve confrontation in fact, the best calendar negotiators are like diplomats. They communicate with grace, knowing how to value everyone's time without devaluing their own priorities. For instance, when two high, ranking stakeholders want the same slot, offer alternate times that show you've considered their needs. Use language that highlights collaboration: "Would you be open to meeting at 2 PM instead? That way, you will have uninterrupted focus, and your message won't be rushed." Strategic negotiation means being firm with time but flexible with solutions.

At the heart of conflict resolution is **relationship intelligence**, the ability to manage people, not just schedules. Every calendar decision impacts someone's workload, energy, or mindset. Understand which personalities are early birds and the ones who like last, minute prep, or which meetings are emotionally charged and should not be stacked. By customizing your calendar strategies to the human beings behind the titles, you reduce not only clashes in time, but emotional friction. And when people feel considered, they feel respected, and they work better. Harmony begins with empathy and ends with thoughtful execution.

Creating harmony in a schedule doesn't mean saying "yes" to everyone. In fact, it often requires a graceful "no." Saying "no" doesn't mean shutting doors, it means opening the right ones at the right time. Learn to say things like, "That sounds like an important conversation. Can we give it the attention it deserves later this week?" or "To protect your deep work time, I've moved this lower, priority meeting to Friday." These micro, decisions, made with tact and clarity, reinforce that you're not just managing the time you're curating it. *Harmony is not a lack of activity; it's the presence of intentional flow.*

One powerful tool in your arsenal is **buffering**. By intentionally placing short gaps between key meetings, you create space to absorb overruns, decompress mentally, and shift focus. These buffers are conflict, preventers in disguise. Don't view them as wasted time, see them as shields protecting your schedule from burnout and bottlenecks. Even five minutes between meetings can mean the difference between arriving scattered and showing up prepared. If you have the power to build a schedule, you also have the responsibility to build in breath.

Finally, empower yourself with the mindset of **calm control.** When a schedule conflict arises, as it inevitably will, respond, don't react. Step back, assess the situation, and make a decision that aligns with priorities, not just pressures. Your value isn't in avoiding all problems; it's in solving them with calm confidence and consistency. The executive who knows you can handle conflict with grace will trust you far more than a calendar, they'll trust you with their time, their rhythm, and ultimately, their success.

Checklist

Anticipation & Audit

Review your executive's calendar **7–14 days ahead** for potential overlaps or tight transitions.

- Check for back, to, back meetings that leave no time for breaks or follow, ups.

- Flag any high, stakes or high, stress meetings that need mental prep or recovery time.

- Confirm that all recurring meetings still serve a current purpose and don't conflict with evolving priorities.

Prioritize & Protect

- Identify and block deep work time or creative flow sessions for your executive.

- Reserve buffer time (5–15 mins) between meetings, especially for important or draining sessions.

- Highlight and protect non, negotiables (board meetings, investor calls, personal/family time).

Negotiate with Tact

- Offer **alternative time slots** when rescheduling requests arise, show flexibility, not just availability.

- Use respectful language like: "Let's protect your focus by shifting this…" or "To avoid overlap, I've proposed…"

- If needed, triage **requests**: Which meetings must stay, which can move, and which can be declined or delegated?

Personalize & Humanize

- Match meeting times to known preferences (e.g., early thinkers, afternoon decision, makers).

- Consider attendees' time zones and availability, especially for international or hybrid teams.

- Anticipate emotional burden: Don't stack intense or draining meetings without recovery space.

Resolve Before It Erupts

- Use **color** codes or tags to immediately identify potential clashes (e.g., red = review needed).

- Communicate changes promptly and clearly to all impacted parties.

- Maintain a "Conflicts to Watch" list and update it daily or weekly.

Maintain Calm Control

- Stay calm under pressure and take a deep breath, then respond to sudden changes as necessary.

- Always assess future implications before shifting any meeting.

- Keep your executive / self, informed of **why** you made changes, not just **what** you changed.

Chapter 5

Rule 5

Navigating External and Internal Meeting Time Zones

The art of calendar management is incomplete without the ability to effectively navigate time zones, especially in today's global business environment. Whether you are scheduling calls with international partners or coordinating internal meetings across multiple regional offices, overlooking time zone differences can lead to confusion, missed appointments, and decreased productivity. Understanding the nuances of time zones and implementing clear practices to address them is crucial for efficient time management and seamless collaboration.

Begin by familiarizing yourself thoroughly with your calendar software's time zone settings. Modern tools like Outlook, Google Calendar, and Apple Calendar offer built, in time zone conversion functionalities. Ensure your calendar settings clearly display event times in both your local time zone and the participants' local zones. Consistently double, check these settings, particularly during daylight saving transitions, to prevent scheduling errors.

Secondly, standardized meeting practices should be created around time zone communication. Clearly state the meeting time with explicit time zone references when inviting participants. Avoid ambiguities by mentioning both your time zone and that of your attendees. For example, instead of simply stating, "Meeting at 10 AM," specify, "Meeting at 10 AM EST (3 PM GMT)." This habit minimizes confusion, reduces follow, up queries, and ensures all attendees arrive prepared and punctual.

Developing a system to accommodate different time zones is equally very important. Consider rotating meeting times periodically to fairly distribute the inconvenience among international teams. For instance, if recurring meetings typically favor a particular region's working hours, periodically schedule them at alternative times to demonstrate equity and inclusivity. This approach not only fosters goodwill but also boosts participation and engagement across geographically dispersed teams.

Proactively managing expectations and setting boundaries regarding availability is another critical component of effective time zone navigation. Communicate your core working hours clearly to colleagues and partners in different regions. Leverage tools and techniques such as automatic out, of, office notifications, clearly defined response, time expectations, and boundary, setting practices to protect your personal and professional time. Doing helps boost productivity, and it also promotes a healthy work, life balance.

Lastly, keep cultural awareness in mind. Being mindful of local holidays, workweek variations, and customary working hours helps in scheduling meetings that respect cultural sensitivities and practical constraints. Employing calendar integrations or referencing global holiday databases can simplify this process significantly. Ultimately, mastering the management of external and internal meeting time zones ensures smoother operations, better interpersonal relationships, and a cohesive global workflow.

I have included some tips that will help you better organize your calendar with some effective Time Zone management skills.

Checklist

Know Your Time Zones

- Identify your local time zone and your executive's primary time zone.

- List all time zones relevant to your team, clients, and key stakeholders.

- Bookmark or download a reliable world clock or time zone converter app (e.g., Time and Date, World Time Buddy).

Schedule with Precision

- Always check the time zone of the meeting initiator before sending a calendar invite.

- Enable time zone support in your calendar settings (e.g., Google Calendar, Outlook).

- Use the "propose new time" feature tactfully when you spot a clash due to time zone differences.

Clear Communication

- Always include both time zones (yours and theirs) in meeting invitations and confirmation emails.

- Add a time zone conversion table in agendas for international participants.

- Including a disclaimer in recurring meeting invites noting that times may shift with daylight saving changes.

Anticipation & Adapt

- Know the daylight, saving schedules of all key regions you collaborate with.

- Adjust recurring meetings well in advance when seasonal time changes are approaching.

- Use floating time zones for frequent travelers or executives on the move.

Prevent Mishaps

- Double, check time zones before sending high, level invites (especially C, suite, or board meetings).

- Confirm the final time with all attendees at least 24 hours before the meeting.

- Keep a "Time Zone Risk Log" for countries or regions that frequently change policies.

Bonus Action:

- Have a visual world clock on your desk or digital dashboard.

- Use AI tools or scheduling assistants that factor in time zone differences automatically.

- Set up alerts for overlapping hours across global teams (for real, time collaboration windows).

Chapter 6

Rule 6

Master Recurring Meetings and Follow, Up

Balancing and Accountability in Your Calendar

Recurring meetings are the heartbeat of a well, organized calendar when strategically managed. They serve as the anchors around which priorities, projects, and performance can align. Whether it's a weekly leadership sync, a monthly financial review, or a daily stand, up, these meetings provide structure and momentum. However, when poorly managed, recurring meetings can become timewasters, suffocating life out of your schedule and leaving participants disengaged. The key here is intentionality, each recurring meeting must have a defined purpose, measurable outcomes, and room for adaptation.

Before a meeting is set on autopilot, ask yourself these three critical questions: Does this meeting still serve a clear objective? Are the right people in the room? And is the frequency appropriate for the agenda? It is astonishing how often meetings continue simply because "we've always done it this way." Calendar mastery begins with the courage to reassess and revise. Cancel what's redundant. Merge what overlaps. Refine what lacks focus. This way, your calendar doesn't just track time, it reflects purpose.

One powerful trick for recurring meetings is to give them a theme. For example, a weekly team check, in might rotate focus areas, week one: wins and roadblocks; week two: project updates; week three: innovation spotlight. Themes introduce freshness, reduce repetition, and ensure different facets of work get attention. Additionally, pre, assigning meeting leads can empower team members and create a sense of shared ownership. Delegation through recurring rhythms cultivates a culture of responsibility and inclusiveness.

Follow, ups are where many calendars break down. A productive meeting without proper follow, through is like planting seeds and forgetting to water them. Masterful calendar managers build in time for post, meeting actions. After every key discussion, allocate 15–30 minutes for notes, email summaries, and task delegation. Better still, create a recurring calendar block labeled "Meeting Follow, Up Hour." This small habit drastically improves accountability and ensures ideas move from discussion to execution.

Technology is your trusted ally when it comes to making recurring meetings smarter, not harder. Use scheduling tools that automatically generate follow, up reminders, auto, send notes, or even track decisions made in the meeting. Integrate your calendar with task management apps like Asana, Trello, or Click Up, to bridge the gap between meetings and outcomes. For high, level executives, having an assistant who can manage this integration is a game, changer. They become not just a scheduler but a strategic partner, ensuring continuity and execution.

Timing is everything. When scheduling recurring meetings, always consider the energy rhythms of the team. Monday mornings may not be ideal for creative brainstorming. Friday afternoons may not inspire action plans. Pay attention to time zones, cultural holidays, and personal workloads. A well, timed recurring meeting is one person who shows up to prepare and present. A poorly timed one becomes just another obligation to endure.

In the end, recurring meetings and follow, ups are not just about structure, they are about flow. They are how a calendar breathes, how teams align, and how progress is sustained. When done well, they create a cadence that reduces chaos and boosts clarity. So, let each meeting be intentional. Let each follow, up be purposeful. And let your calendar become not just a record of meetings, but a living system of results.

Checklist

Setting Up Strategic Recurring Meetings

- Have I clearly defined the purpose of each recurring meeting?

- Is the current frequency (daily/weekly/monthly) still appropriate?

- Are all attendees essential, or can the invite list be streamlined?

- Have you assigned rotating roles (host, note, taker, timekeeper) to boost engagement?

- Does the meeting include a theme or focus area to keep it fresh and productive?

Audit & Optimize

- Reviewing all current recurring meetings, are there any I can cancel, combine, or replace?

- Do these meetings align with current goals and team priorities?

- Have I built in buffer time before and after meetings to avoid overload?

- Are there meetings happening "out of habit" rather than necessity?

Mastering the Follow, Up

- Have I blocked 15–30 minutes after each key meeting for follow, up tasks?

- Do I summarize key points, decisions, and action items immediately after the meeting?

- Am I sending follow, up emails or messages to keep everyone on the same page?

- Are deadlines, owners, and next steps clearly documented and tracked?

Tech & Tools Integration

- Am I using automation tools to schedule reminders and follow, ups?

- Have I integrated my calendar with task managers like Asana, Click Up, or Trello?

- Do I use AI meeting assistants (like Otter or Fireflies) to auto, generate notes and action lists?

Time with Intention

- Are my recurring meetings scheduled based on peak team productivity times?

- Have I considered global time zones and cultural differences?

- Do I pause reassessing meetings every quarter to keep them relevant?

Chapter 7

Rule 7

Clear and Concise Calendar Management

No Place for Ambiguity in a High, Performance Schedule

Clarity is one of the most underrated calendar superpowers. A cluttered or vague calendar is like a disorganized closet, you waste time searching, second, guessing, and misplacing important pieces. When your calendar entries are vague ("Catch, up," "Call," "Meeting"), you're creating confusion, not clarity. On the other hand, specific and concise calendar entries immediately communicate what needs to happen, who's involved, and what's expected. Precision isn't just polite, it's powerful.

Effective calendar management starts with **naming conventions.** A well, labeled event tells a story in just a few words: "Weekly Ops Review – Team Leads Only (Zoom)" or "Board Meeting Prep – Internal Strategy Sync w/ Sarah." Compare that to simply writing "Meeting." Which one empowers you to show up prepared? Use prefixes (e.g., "1:1", "Team," "Client," "Prep"), include locations or platforms, and specify the people involved. The goal is to reduce friction and increase flow.

Color coding is another game, changing technique. Assign specific colors to categories, green for revenue, generating activities, blue for strategic planning, yellow for personal or wellness time. With a single glance, you can assess whether your week is aligned with your priorities or if it needs adjusting. Visual clarity boosts mental clarity, and this simple method helps ensure you're not crowding your calendar with low, impact obligations.

Another strategy that people often undermine is the power

of descriptions and attachments. When adding events, use the description box to include relevant documents, agendas, links, or context. This removes the need to dig through emails right before a call and gives your future self a head start. For executive assistants, this is a non, negotiable habit that enables executives to walk into meetings fully equipped, increasing confidence and performance.

When collaborating with others, be sure to respect their time and understand them, too. Avoid internal shorthand and abbreviations that others may not recognize. Instead, use professional, universal language that translates across departments and time zones. Your calendar is not your personal tool, it is a medium of communication shared with others. Every event title, note, or time slot should reflect thoughtfulness and clarity.

In a high, performing workplace, time is of the essential, and your calendar is the logbook. Mastering clear and concise calendar entries means fewer missed appointments, reduced back, and, forth, and more time spent on high, value tasks. It's a practice that builds trust, demonstrates professionalism, and keeps you in control. The clearer your calendar, the sharper your execution. Never underestimate the power of a well, written calendar entry, it's the first step toward a productive day.

Checklist:

Label with Purpose

- Do I use specific, action, oriented titles for all calendar entries? Example: "Team Check, in: Marketing Q2 Goals" instead of just "Meeting"

- Have I included the names of participants and context in the title when necessary?

- Do I use consistent prefixes like "1:1," "Client," "Internal," or "Review" to sort and scan events quickly?

Color, Code Like a Pro

- Have I assigned colors to key categories (e.g., Admin, Strategy, Personal, Revenue)?

- Is my calendar visually balanced between deep work, meetings, and personal time?

- Are high, priority, or high, impact activities clearly visible at a glance?

Add Supporting Details

- Do I use the description box to include relevant links, agendas, and documents?

- Have I attached files or prep notes to meetings requiring prior review?

- Is each recurring event documented with expectations, frequency, and outcomes?

Review for Consistency

- Have I reviewed my calendar this week to clean up vague or outdated event titles?

- Is there any duplication or overlap that needs to be merged or canceled?

- Do my calendar entries reflect my goals and responsibilities accurately?

Make It Collaborative

- Do I use clear, universal language that others can understand quickly?

- Have I verified that the invitees have access to all necessary materials before meetings?

- Am I using calendar notes to reduce back, and, forth

emails for scheduling?

Best Practices

- Do I set reminders that give me enough time to prepare mentally and logistically?

- Have I blocked time for weekly calendar cleanup and reflection?

- Am I intentional about how I present my availability to others (e.g., using working hours, status updates)?

- Bonus Action Set a recurring Friday afternoon reminder titled "Calendar Clean, Up & Clarity Check" to stay ahead of clutter.

Chapter 8

Rule 8

Master Your Tools and Technology

Upgrade Your Efficiency, One Click at a Time

In today's digital world, your calendar is more than a planner, it's your **productivity dashboard**, your accountability partner, and your silent assistant; however, it can only serve you well if you know how to harness its full potential. Mastering your tools and technology isn't just an added advantage, it is essential for anyone who wants to operate at peak performance. Whether you're managing your own time or supporting a high, level executive, the ability to optimize calendar tools gives you an unmistakable edge.

Too often, people use only the basic features of tools like Google Calendar, Outlook, or Apple Calendar, leaving powerful functions untouched. These platforms offer automated reminders, color coding, time zone support, recurring scheduling, integration with task managers, and even AI, based suggestions. When these features are configured properly, they not only keep you organized but **proactively prevent conflicts,** reduce manual tasks, and saves you from mental stress. The secret? Stop reacting to your calendar, start commanding it.

Integration is one of the most overlooked opportunities in calendar technology. Syncing your calendar with tools like Trello, Asana, Slack, Zoom, or Microsoft Teams allows seamless flow between scheduling and execution. For example, connecting Zoom to your calendar can auto, generate meeting links and insert them directly into invites. Syncing with task managers ensures that every scheduled meeting has a follow, up action attached. This kind of **workflow synchronization** turns your calendar into a command center for your day.

The best executive assistants and calendar, savvy professionals always embrace automation. Tools like Calendly, Doodle, and Motion eliminate the back, and, forth of scheduling and allow stakeholders to book time based on availability rules you define. Smart scheduling links can limit how many meetings can be booked in a day, enforce buffer times, and respect personal time blocks. These tools reduce burnout, reinforce boundaries, and **put you back in control of your schedule.**

Mastering tools isn't just about the tech, it's about developing systems. You need a consistent routine for reviewing calendar invites, confirming meeting logistics, archiving past events, and checking for upcoming conflicts. Create a 5, minute daily check, in, a 30, minute weekly review, and a monthly audit to assess how your tools are serving you. This regular practice ensures you're not just adding events but building a **strategy of time.**

Finally, remember technology is only powerful when paired with intention. Mastery doesn't come from knowing every feature; it comes from using the right features **consistently and intentionally**. Choose tools that match your work style, learn them deeply, and set rules for how you'll use them. When your tools serve your priorities and protect your peace, you've moved from digital overwhelm to calendar command, and that's where the art of Calendar mastery truly begins.

Checklist

Calendar Audit: What's in Your Digital Toolbox?

List the calendar apps and scheduling tools you currently use

Identify duplicate tools or unused features

Rank each tool: How well does it support your time, blocking, notifications, and sync needs?

Sync It Up – Don't Let Gaps Cost You Time

Confirm your calendar is synced across all devices (phone, desktop, tablet)

Check integration with your email, project management, and video conferencing tools

Test syncing to catch double, bookings or time zone errors

Master Your Notifications – Become the Boss of Your Alerts

Customize alerts for each meeting type (e.g., 15 minutes before internal, 30 minutes for external)

Set non, negotiable "do not disturb" hours

Use sound/vibration settings to match your work focus mode

Automate the Repetitive – Delegate to Tech

Create templates for recurring meetings and follow, ups

Use scheduling links (e.g., Calendly or Google Meet) to reduce email back, and, forth

Automate follow, up reminders for important tasks or deliverables

Learn Shortcuts & Features You're Underusing

Identify at least 3 features you've never used on your primary calendar tool

Watch a 5, minute tutorial video on optimizing those features

Challenge: Can you set up a color, coded view, or smart labels for different meeting types?

Backups & Data Security: Guard Your Schedule Like Gold

Check if your calendar data is backed up automatically

Review your sharing permissions, who can see/edit your

calendar?

Add a secure password or authentication tool if managing executive schedules

Evaluation & Monthly Upgrade

Set a 30, minute monthly slot for a calendar tool review

Ask: What's helping? What's slowing me down? What needs updating?

Keep a "tech Wishlist" for tools you want to explore

Bonus Action:

Choose one new tech feature this week that you will fully master and apply. Whether it's a shortcut, plugin, or calendar integration , make it work for you, not the other way around!

Chapter 9

Rule 9

Anticipating and Adjusting for Last, Minute Changes

A proactive mindset keeps you and your calendar's reputation intact.

Last, minute changes are an inevitable part of a highly functional calendar. Meetings get moved, priorities shift, and urgent requests show up without warning, but a true calendar master doesn't crumble under the pressure of unexpected change. They anticipate them. Anticipation is a skill. It's about knowing where potential fires might start and setting up guardrails before they even spark. Whether you're managing your own schedule or your executive's, expecting the unexpected is not paranoia, it's professionalism.

A great anticipator develops a radar for potential disruptions. Do you know which stakeholders are prone to reschedules? Are there recurring patterns of unpredictability with certain projects or departments? Do you track external events, such as industry conferences, school holidays, or travel seasons, that could affect availability? When you train your mind to look beyond the surface of a calendar entry, you develop foresight. And foresight is power.

Adjustments, however, are where your strategy truly shines. Anyone can react; few can respond with poise and purpose. Adjusting for a last, minute change doesn't mean simply moving boxes on a screen, it's about rebalancing priorities. A 2 PM board meeting moved to noon? That means your prep session must shift, too. That internal check, in? Maybe it becomes an email summary or a quick Teams message instead. Being agile while maintaining intention is what separates you from being just "busy" to being brilliantly effective.

Technology can help, but the human touch is irreplaceable. Set protocols in place: automated reminders, confirmation messages, and a dashboard that highlights potential conflicts. But don't stop there, communicate with empathy. If a team member's meeting is bumped, please acknowledge the inconvenience, and offer clarity. If an executive's prep time vanishes due to an urgent call, suggest a focused follow, up slot or support material to keep them sharp. People remember how you handle changes and not that they just happened.

Most importantly, give yourself grace and build in buffers. Time, blocking is great, but don't stack your day so tightly that a minor shift causes a major meltdown. Create space around high, stakes commitments and allow transition time between tasks. This not only supports your mental clarity but ensures that when the curveballs come (and they will), you're not forced to choose between two important things, you're equipped to pivot smoothly.

In the end, calendar mastery is not about building the perfect plan, it's about creating a flexible one. ***Life is dynamic, work is unpredictable, and mastery lies in movement.*** The ability to anticipate and adjust with confidence doesn't just protect your productivity, it elevates your reputation as someone who is reliable, resilient, and ready. Be calm in the calendar chaos. Be the one who turns disruption into a display of excellence.

Checklist:

Anticipate. Adjust. Overcome Every Obstacle

Turn surprises into strengths with strategic foresight and flexibility.

- ❖ **Build Your Calendar Radar**
  - o Identify frequent reschedulers (clients, departments, or teammates)
  - o Review the past 30 days, how many meetings were moved or cancelled?
  - o Note any recurring seasonal or industry, related disruptions to anticipate next time

- ❖ **Creating a Flex, Buffer Strategy**
  - o Block 15–30 mins of transition time between major meetings
  - o Add "contingency slots" in your weekly plan for overflow or urgent tasks
  - o Label high, priority, non, negotiable meetings with a visual cue (e.g., 🔒 or ⭐)

- ❖ **Sharpen Your Adjustment Mindset**
  - o Reframe calendar shifts as strategic pivots instead of disruptions
  - o Practice making quick decisions: What can move? What must stay?
  - o Create a mental checklist for triaging changes (Impact? Urgency? Stakeholders?)

- ❖ **Use Tech to Stay Ahead**
  - o Set up calendar notifications for meetings with high change risk

- o Automate confirmation requests 24–48 hours before key appointments
- o Sync calendar with mobile devices for real, time access and updates

❖ **Communicating with Clarity & Compassion**

- o When changes occur, notify all affected parties immediately
- o Offer revised options, alternative formats (call instead of Zoom?), or prep summaries
- o Acknowledge the inconvenience, your empathy is your leadership currency

❖ **Debrief and Learn**

- o At the end of the week, review:
  - What changes happened?
  - How well did you adapt?
  - What could be improved next time?
- o Document lessons learned in a "Calendar Insights" journal

❖ **Bonus Challenge:**

Run a 5, day "Pivot Like a Pro" challenge.

Each day, identify a potential disruption and write down your ideal proactive response. End the week with a personal playbook for handling last, minute changes with ease.

Chapter 10

Rule 10

Confidentiality & Discretion – Learn to Say No with Finesse

Protecting time, trust, and truth with wisdom and grace.

In the world of calendar management, especially for executive assistants and high, level professionals, **confidentiality is not an option; it is foundational.** Every meeting you schedule, every invite you send, and every note you jot may carry sensitive, strategic, or private information. Whether it is an internal performance review, an investor meeting, or a merger conversation, your calendar isn't just a time grid, it is a vault of trust. Understanding what to share, what to conceal, and how to do both gracefully is what makes you not just organized, but indispensable.

Discretion goes beyond protecting private details, it's about knowing **what to say, when to say it, how to say it, and who to say it to.** That might mean avoiding certain calendar subject lines, using abbreviations for private meetings, or setting permissions so that only appropriate eyes see what's necessary. You're not just guarding time, you're guarding reputations, strategies, and even careers. A well, kept calendar should not reveal more than it needs to. Think of it as a well, tailored suit: structured, professional, and never revealing too much.

Confidentiality also comes with the responsibility of knowing when and how to **say no.** Be aware that not every meeting request deserves a slot, and not every person asking for "just 15 minutes" should get it. Mastering the art of saying no without sounding dismissive is a skill that separates the reactive from the strategic. It's not about rejection; it is about redirection. Instead of a blunt "no," try: *"That time is already committed, can I offer a later slot?"* or *"Let me circle back once we* *prioritize current deliverables."* Power lies in protecting your time without burning bridges.

One of the most powerful forms of discretion is **silent leadership,** the kind that's not loud but deeply respected. You know who's meeting with who, what's truly urgent, and which "urgent" isn't urgent at all. You become the quiet orchestrator behind the scenes. This quiet authority earns you influence because people trust you. In addition, trust is the currency that buys access, credibility, and long, term success in any professional environment.

In a fast, paced world full of oversharing and calendar clutter, becoming known as someone who can be **counted on to protect time and information** is your legacy. Your calendar should be clean, clear, and confidential, not just for aesthetics, but for security and sustainability. As you implement everything from this book, remember that it's not just about being efficient. It's about being *effective, ethical, and empowering.* Your discretion is your dignity in action.

Let this final chapter serve as a reminder: **Time is sacred. Trust is sacred.** And when you master both, you don't just manage calendars, you shape cultures. You create safe, structured environments where people can operate at their best, without fear that their time or intentions will be mishandled. You set the standard for how respect, professionalism, and grace show up on the page of a calendar. That's legacy, level work.

So, as this chapter ends, carry forward the responsibility of calendar mastery with pride. Every meeting you set, every time block you protect, and every "no" you say with kindness is a building block of a more efficient, empowered world. You're not just managing time; you're mastering life. And that's a legacy worth scheduling.

Checklist:

❖ **Confidentiality Protocols**

- o Use professional and discreet subject lines for sensitive meetings

- o Set appropriate calendar visibility settings (private vs. public)

- o Avoid putting confidential notes in shared calendar descriptions

- o Use password protection and secure platforms for executive meetings

❖ **Discretion in Action**

- o Identify which meetings require anonymity or special handling

- o Keep executive and high, stake conversations need, to, know only

- o Practice discretion when discussing schedule changes with others

- o Refrain from over, explaining reschedules, focus on impact, not detail

❖ **Saying No with Finesse**

- o Use polite deflection phrases:

- o "That time is already allocated"

- o "Let me propose another slot"

- o "We're focusing on critical deliverables right now"

- o Always offer an alternative or future follow-up where possible

- o Balance firmness with friendliness in your tone

- o Trust your judgment, protecting time is protecting

performance

❖ **Establishing Calendar Boundaries**

- o Review your calendar weekly for overexposure to unnecessary meetings

- o Block "sacred time" for deep work, rest, and strategic planning

- o Create a policy for external requests and referrals

- o Practice saying "no" at least once this week to protect your priorities

Affirmations for Calendar Confidence & Legacy Leadership

❖ I am the guardian of my time, and I protect it with wisdom and clarity.

❖ I handle every meeting and message with integrity, purpose, and professionalism.

❖ My calendar reflects intention, not just activity.

❖ I say "no" with kindness, and "yes" with conviction.

❖ I am trusted because I am consistent, confidential, and composed.

❖ I create space not just for meetings, but for meaning.

❖ I am a calendar master, shaping not just schedules, but futures.

Conclusion

As you turn the final page of *Calendar Mastery*, you have done more than read a book; you've embraced a new standard. You are now equipped with the tools, principles, and mindset of someone who doesn't just manage time but rules over it with clarity and intention. Whether you support a high, level executive or lead your own schedule, you've stepped into the role of time architect, strategic, thoughtful, and future, focused.

Remember, mastery isn't a destination, it's a discipline. Your calendar will still face disruptions, priorities will still shift, and life is still going to happen. What sets you apart now is your ability to respond with foresight, structure, and grace. With every buffer you build, every "no" you say with confidence, and every moment of protected focus, you reinforce the habits of someone who values both time and purpose.

This is your invitation to go beyond the pages. Review your current calendar with fresh eyes. Audit your meetings and reevaluate your goals. Apply one new strategy each week for the next 10 weeks. Share what you've learned with others who need it. And most of all, don't underestimate the ripple effect of managing time well, it elevates not only your work but the people and priorities you serve.

Let this book be a beginning, not an ending. You now have the golden key to calendar management, you are now equipped to create balance, lead with intentionality, and protect what matters most. The power is in your hands, and your schedule. Go forward boldly, and plan with purpose. Leave behind a legacy.

www.ingramcontent.com/pod-product-compliance
Lightning Source LLC
Chambersburg PA
CBHW071215300726
48975CB00004B/1323